For Ellen, Emily, and Julia.

Little Boost is published by
Picture Window Books
A Capstone Imprint
1710 Roe Crest Drive
North Mankato, Minnesota 56003
www.capstonepub.com

Library of Congress Cataloging-in-Publication Data
Bracken, Beth.
  The little bully / by Beth Bracken ; illustrated by Jennifer Bell.
      p. cm. -- (Little boost)
  Summary: When Fred makes fun of Billy at school, Billy has to
learn how to deal with his friend's bullying.
  ISBN 978-1-4048-6795-6 (library binding)
  1. Bullying--Juvenile fiction. 2. Schools--Juvenile fiction.
3. Friendship--Juvenile fiction. 4. Human behavior--Juvenile
fiction. [1. Bullies--Fiction. 2. Schools--Fiction. 3. Friendship--
Fiction.] I. Bell, Jennifer A., ill. II. Title. III. Series: Little boost.
  PZ7.B6989Li 2012
  [E]--dc23
                                    2011029540

Designer: Emily Harris

Printed in the United States of America
in North Mankato, Minnesota.
102011   006405CGS12

The Little Bully

by Beth Bracken

illustrated by Jennifer A. Bell

PICTURE WINDOW BOOKS
a capstone imprint

Billy was a cool kid. He was nice to people. He was nice to animals. He had a nice smile, and he was very polite.

Billy had a lot of friends, and nobody was ever mean to him.

Well, nobody except **Fred**.

Fred could see the tiniest stain on Billy's shirt.

"Billy spills EVERYTHING! What a slob!"

If Billy made one mistake when he was writing,
Fred would point and laugh.

"Billy can't even write his name!"

For show-and-tell, Billy brought a drawing of his family.
He thought it was pretty great.

But Fred couldn't stop laughing when he saw it.

"You used so much pink. That's a color for girls!"

Billy tried to stand up for himself. But no matter what he said,
Fred would just laugh.

It made Billy feel **horrible**.

Billy started to think
he wasn't **smart**.

Or **funny**.

Or **nice** to look at.

Billy started to think that **nobody** liked him.

Billy didn't want to go to school anymore. But he didn't want to tell his mom or dad the real reason.

Instead, he said, "School is **dumb**. I just want to stay home."

"Going to school is your job," Dad told him.

"It's important for you to do your job," Mom said.

So Billy kept going to school, and Fred kept teasing him.

One day, Billy wore his favorite shirt to school. Of course, Fred made fun of it.

"You're wearing a baby shirt!"

Billy knew his shirt wasn't a baby shirt. He had a baby sister. Babies hardly even wore shirts. They usually wore pajamas, and they definitely didn't wear cool orange shirts with trucks on them.

Before Billy said anything, he looked at Fred.

Fred's shirt had a bear on it, he had paint on his pants, and his shoes were untied.

Fred didn't have **any other friends** besides Billy, and it would be easy to make fun of him.

But Billy knew Fred's shoes were untied because it was hard to keep shoes tied.

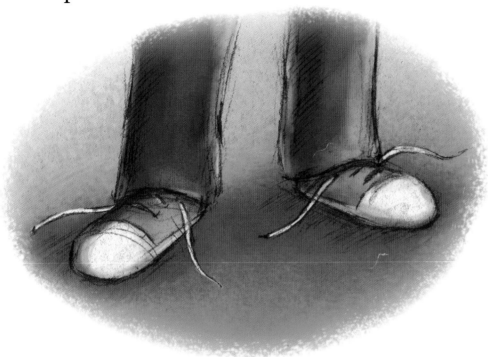

He liked Fred's bear shirt.

And they had been painting that morning, so **everyone** had paint on their pants.

So Billy tried something new.

"I like my shirt," he said bravely. "It's **not** a baby shirt."

"Well, your pants have paint all over them," Fred said.

"So do yours. And if you keep being mean to me, I won't play with you," Billy said.

Billy knew nobody else wanted to play with Fred.

Fred knew it, too.

After that, Fred wasn't mean to Billy. In fact, once he stopped being mean, Fred became a really **cool** guy.

Just like Billy.